LOVE
AND
ROAST
CHICKEN

To Chris,
my sturdy traveling
companion

Muchas gracias to Edwin Sulca for telling this story at our
dinner table, for his constant hospitality in Ayacucho, and
for inspiring so many with his courage and creativity.

Abrazos to Martha Castellanos for her firsthand expertise in
Andean language and culture, her kind advice, and for her
warm encouragement along the way.

LOVE AND ROAST CHICKEN

A TRICKSTER TALE FROM THE ANDES MOUNTAINS

BARBARA KNUTSON

CAROLRHODA BOOKS, INC. / MINNEAPOLIS

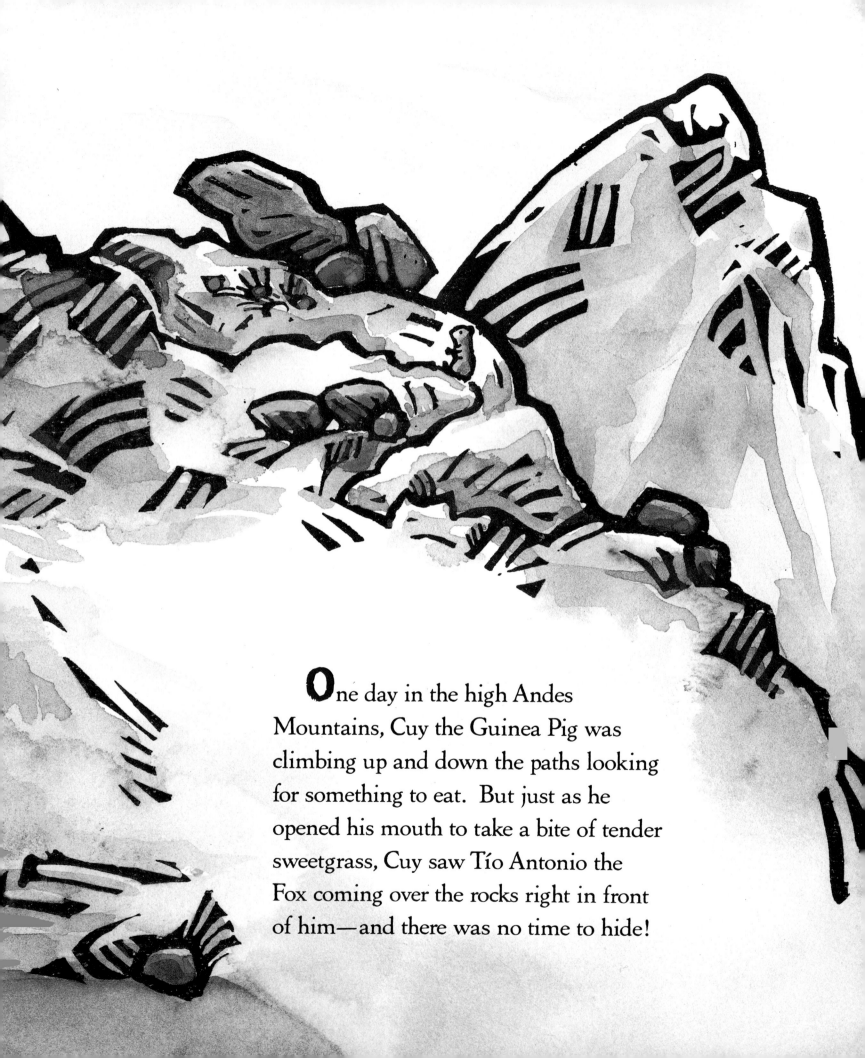

One day in the high Andes Mountains, Cuy the Guinea Pig was climbing up and down the paths looking for something to eat. But just as he opened his mouth to take a bite of tender sweetgrass, Cuy saw Tío Antonio the Fox coming over the rocks right in front of him—and there was no time to hide!

Cuy thought fast. He squeezed under the edge
of a great rock and pressed up with his arms.

"Aha! Dinner!" snarled Fox, ready to pounce.

"Tío Antonio!" cried Cuy. "Haven't you heard?
The sky is falling!"

"Nonsense!" growled Tío Antonio, but he couldn't help looking up. "It looks the same as always!"

"That's because I'm holding it up with this rock," said Cuy. "I've been here all day, and I need to go to the bathroom. Please, will you hold the rock for just a moment?"

Fox looked up again. It would be terrible if the sky fell. He crouched under the rock and pushed up with his front legs.

"Don't let go," warned Cuy, "or we will all be squashed flat." He disappeared behind some bushes and scurried off to look for more food.

By sunset, Tío Antonio couldn't hold his arms up any longer. "I have to let go, even if the sky falls!" He ducked and let go.

Nothing happened. The rock and the sky stayed where they had always been.

"I'll get that guinea pig!" barked Fox, and he bounded down the trail.

Cuy had just found another patch
of sweetgrass when he saw Fox coming.
Instantly, he started digging into the
side of the hill.

"This time I've got you!" said Tío
Antonio, and he grabbed Cuy's leg.

"*Amigo mío!*" yelped Cuy. "Don't you know the world is ending tonight in a rain of fire? Help me dig a safe den!"

"I'm not going to believe you this time!" declared Fox.

"All right," said Guinea Pig. "Don't blame me when your whiskers are on fire."

Fox trembled. What if this were true?
He shoved Cuy aside and crawled into the
dug-out hole. "Well then, this den is for me,
compadre. Go dig your own!"

Cuy sighed. *"Está bien!* I'll even pile some rocks in front of the door to keep you safe from sparks. When the world ends, remember I was your last friend."

Tío Antonio huddled at the back of the den and waited. The end of the world! No more dancing by moonlight with the village girls. No more chicken dinners from the farmer's flock. But could this just be another trick? He peered through the rocks covering the entrance.

Fuego! Flames crackled and smoked on the other side. What a good thing he was safe!

When morning came at last, the flames were gone. Tío Antonio pushed away the rocks to see what the end of the world looked like.

The sun was shining, a condor was soaring over the mountains, and down in the valley Florinda, the farmer's daughter, was planting potatoes. In front of Fox's den lay a pile of ashes from Guinea Pig's fire.

"Cuy!" howled Fox. "Next time, I'll eat you on the spot!"

But Cuy had a plan. "I'm going where there's plenty of food and someone who always chases Fox away," he decided. He put on a hat and a poncho and went down the mountain to knock on the farmer's door.

"*Buenos días, Papay,*" said Cuy. "Need any help with the alfalfa?"

"What a small man," thought the farmer, "but I do need help."

"*Bueno,*" he said. "You can start right away."

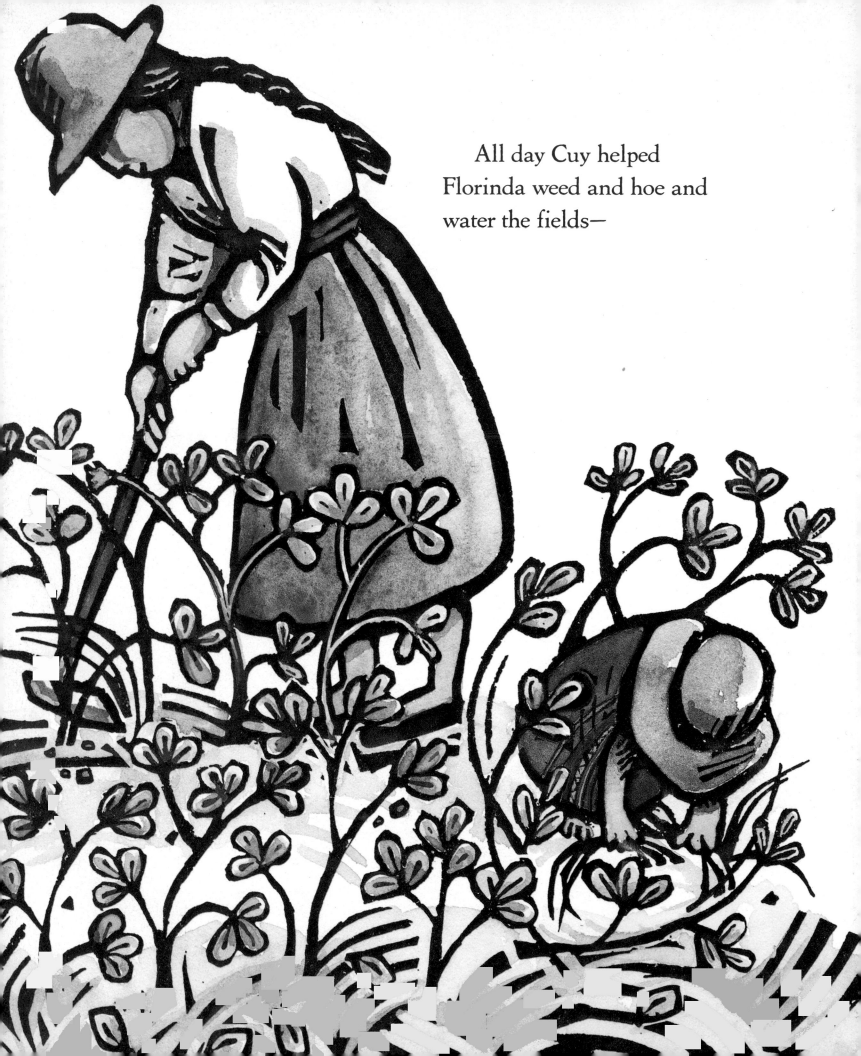

All day Cuy helped
Florinda weed and hoe and
water the fields—

but all night he feasted on fresh alfalfa. "All this food and no Fox in sight—I'm going to stay here the rest of my life!" he decided.

By the third day, the farmer noticed something
was wrong. "Who is stealing all my alfalfa?" he
wondered. "I'd better make it look like someone is
guarding the field."

He shaped a little person out of clay and covered
it with sticky sap from the eucalyptus tree. He
propped it up in the field and went to bed.

In the middle of the night, Cuy crept out for a snack,
but someone had gotten there before him.

"*Buenas noches!* Are you a friend of Florinda's?" he
said. The visitor said nothing. "I said, hello!" Cuy
reached out to shake her hand. His paw stuck.

"Oho, so you want to hold my hand!" said Cuy. He patted her on the shoulder with his other paw, but that one stuck too.

"*Caramba!* Let go!" Guinea Pig said. "If you don't let go, I'll kick you!" But the person didn't say a word, and she didn't let go.

Cuy kicked hard with his right foot—which stuck. Then he kicked with his left foot—and that stuck too.

"How rude!" he cried. "Let go, or I'll hit you with my head!" But when he did that, his head stuck too. "LET ME GO!" shouted Cuy so loudly that the farmer woke up and ran outside.

"*Qué tramposo!* What a rascal! You're not a farmworker, you're a guinea pig!" cried the farmer. "And you've been eating all my alfalfa! Well, Florinda loves to eat roast guinea pig, and tomorrow we will eat YOU!"

He pulled Cuy free from the sticky gum doll. Then he tied him to the eucalyptus tree and went back to bed.

"It can't get any worse than this!"
thought Cuy. But here came Tío Antonio
sneaking toward the chicken coop.

"Well, well!" said Fox. "I was
looking for chicken dinner, but here is
my appetizer!" He came closer, the
moonlight glinting on his sharp teeth.
"Why are you tied up?"

Guinea Pig gulped. Everyone wanted to eat him. "Oh, Tío Antonio!" he gasped, thinking fast. "It's all because of love and roast chicken."

Fox perked up his ears. "Those are my favorite subjects."

Cuy put his paw over his heart. "You know the farmer's daughter, Florinda? She wants to marry me. But the trouble is, she eats chicken every single day. Can you imagine?"

Fox imagined it.

"But I am a vegetarian!" declared Cuy. "They've tied me up until I promise to marry Florinda and eat big plates of roast chicken every day! What am I going to do?"

"*Pobrecito,*" said Tío Antonio, licking his lips. "I hate to see you suffer. It will be a hard life for me, but just to help you, I will take your place."

"Really?" said Cuy. "You are very kind."

So Fox untied Cuy. Then Cuy tied Tío Antonio to the tree and slipped back into the alfalfa field for one last feast.

The next morning, the farmer came out to untie his dinner. To his surprise, he found a fox.

"What now? Another disguise?" The farmer picked up a stick.

"Oh no, *Papay,* don't hit me!" said Tío Antonio.
"I promise to eat one of your chickens every day of the year!"

"*¿Cómo?*" cried the farmer.

"Of course, *Papay,*" Tío Antonio added quickly, "I also plan
to marry your daughter."

"*¿COMO?*" spat the farmer, and he raised the stick over his head. As fast as he could, Tío Antonio explained what Cuy had said.

"You believed a story like that? How foolish!"
The farmer laughed until the tears ran down his
cheeks. *"Qué ridículo!"*

While the farmer laughed, Fox bit clean through the rope and scrambled over the field wall. "CUY!" he howled as he ran. "You will never trick me again!"

And to make sure that was true, he stayed away from Cuy for a long, long time.

Author's Note

I lived in Peru for two years while my husband taught at a school in Lima, the capital city. From Lima we could visit the ocean, the desert, the rain forest, and the great, high, snowy Andes Mountains (in brown on the map) that stretch down the west side of South America. We loved hiking and camping in the Andes. I still remember how tiny I felt at the foot of those huge mountains and how many stars we could see at night. On my travels, I met many friendly people (and a fox and some guinea pigs). I also learned many stories, including trickster tales that reminded me of the ones I know from Africa.

A trickster tale tells about a small animal (or a person) who uses brains instead of force to compete against bigger, fiercer characters. In the Andes, the trickster is often a little gray fox, but one story has a guinea pig hero. I have heard and read this tale many times in Spanish—in a lovely, old Bolivian book; from a Peruvian guide in a mountain town; in a Bolivian children's magazine; and from our friend Edwin Sulca, a Peruvian weaver. It was never told the same way twice! In this book, I have combined and rearranged my favorite versions.

How did a guinea pig get to star in this story? Guinea pigs are part of traditional life in the Andes. They used to run wild in the mountains, like rabbits. Hundreds of years ago, people started raising them for food. In street markets, they still sell guinea pigs for the same purpose—but at least in this story, Cuy wins after all.

New Words to Say

In the Andes, people mix Spanish with the ancient languages of Quechua or Aymara.
The following words are Spanish unless noted otherwise:

amigo mío:	(ah-MEE-goh MEE-oh)	my friend
buenas noches:	(BWAY-nahs NOH-ches)	good evening, good night
bueno:	(BWAY-noh)	good, all right
buenos días:	(BWAY-nohs DEE-ahs)	good morning
caramba:	(cah-RAM-bah)	exclamation of surprise
¿cómo?:	(COH-moh)	what? In Spanish, a question begins and ends with a question mark.
compadre:	(com-PAH-dray)	a form of address to a male friend
cuy:	(KWEE)	guinea pig (Quechua)
está bien:	(es-TAH bee-YEN)	fine, all right
fuego:	(FWAY-goh)	fire
Papay:	(pah-PIE)	a common form of address to a man, similar to "mister" or "sir" (Quechua)
pobrecito:	(poh-bray-SEE-toh)	poor little thing
qué ridículo:	(KAY ree-DEE-coo-loh)	how ridiculous
qué tramposo:	(KAY trahm-POH-soh)	what a trickster
tío:	(TEE-oh)	uncle. Tío Antonio is a traditional Andean name for the fox.

Carolrhoda Books, Inc.
A division of Lerner Publishing Group
241 First Avenue North
Minneapolis, MN 55401 U.S.A.

Website address: www.lernerbooks.com

Library of Congress Cataloging-in-Publication Data

Knutson, Barbara.
   Love and roast chicken : a trickster tale from the Andes Mountains / Barbara Knutson.
     p. cm.
   Summary: In this folktale from the Andes, a clever guinea pig repeatedly outsmarts the fox that wants to eat him for dinner.
   ISBN: 1–57505–657–7 (lib. bdg. : alk. paper)
   1. Indians of South America—Andes Region—Folklore. 2. Guinea pigs—Andes Region—Folklore. 3. Tricksters—Andes Region. [1. Indians of South America—Andes Region—Folklore. 2. Folklore—South America. 3. Tricksters—Folklore.] I. Title.
F2230.1.F6K58 2004
398.2'098'045293592—dc22   2003018045

Manufactured in the United States of America
3 4 5 6 7 8 – JR – 10 09 08 07 06 05